QUEERLY
BELOVED

QUEERLY BELOVED

C A Shepherd

1

Detective Chief Inspector Louise Lavache was a misanthropist – or, in more modern-day parlance – a bitch. There were few members of the human species – male, female or somewhere in between – who did not find themselves objects of her derision. She was thus, unsurprisingly, unattached, since there was not a single person among her acquaintance that she could countenance sharing a fridge with, let alone her heart (and indeed, the feeling was mutual among said acquaintances).

At thirty-eight years old, Lavache had made a rapid ascent to (Acting) DCI grade, aided by a fast-track graduate programme, a lack of romantic entanglements and ensuing by-products, plus the rather fortuitous stress-related heart attack suffered by her predecessor, DCI Mervyn Brumfitt.

Standing at five foot ten, slim in build with short, edgy black hair and a preponderance to swoosh about in a dark trench-coat, she cut a striking, if rather austere, figure. Had she learnt to relax her jawline and break into a smile once in a while, she could have even been attractive. But a sardonic laugh, invariably at someone else's expense, was the closest Lavache came to a smile. She was – to truncate the narrative – thoroughly unpleasant. She also appeared to take perverse pleasure in being dislikeable, a trait that the savvier among Hollingham Police recognised to be a mask for intense self-hatred.

DCI Lavache presided over a team of five at CID within the divisional station of Hollingham, a soulless and ever-expanding commuter town on the Hampshire-Berkshire border. Entrusted to her dubious care was Detective Inspector Gary Oakes, who at ten years Lavache's senior in age, did not find his subordinate role an altogether snug fit. Beneath Gary, though not in the carnal sense (yet) presided Detective Sergeant Sienna Jones. And at the bottom of the heap were Detective Constables Mandeep Kaur and Jack Clements. The names would probably change within a month, however; staff retention was not a forte of Hollingham CID with the thoroughly unpleasant Louise Lavache at its helm. There were signs, however, that County HQ were getting rather fed up of the recent spate of one way secondments out of Hollingham nick.

Gary Oakes, twice divorced but never shy, was a balding forty something, with what little hair there was left on his pallid pate as grey and greasy as the cheap chain store suit he wore day in, day out, earning him the nickname Greasy Oik. He lived alone in Hollingham, but unlike his senior officer, Oakes lived in a soulless new build estate just off the A34 – known locally as the Divorcee & Swingers Estate – and not on the more desirable side of town near the Waitrose 24/7, where the thoroughbreds lived.

His sergeant, Sienna Jones, a recent transfer from South Wales Police, provided a welcome bit of eye candy for the likes of Gary and his heterosexual colleagues at Hollingham Station. Whilst DS Jones had acquired intimate knowledge of several uniformed officers at the station, she had (so far) refused any overtures from members of her own team. She had her professional standards, after all. And there was something ever so sexy about a man in uniform.

Mandeep Kaur, though slight in frame and surprisingly feminine for a female CID officer, was as tough as a pair of steel toe caps. In addition, she had a potty mouth on her that wouldn't have been out of place in a Glasgow shipyard. Her expletive riddled invective frequently caused the fresh-faced Jack Clements to blush, as it did the general public. For that precise reason, Kaur was banned from television and radio interviews, in these days of viral social media postings, however minor the news outlet.

Clements would have made a textbook baby-faced assassin, had there been anything assassinous about him. As it was, he was a somewhat of a wimp, press-ganged to sign up for the force by his uncle, the recently retired Chief Constable of Hollingham and District, Neville Clements.

Frequently the butt of Louise Lavache's sardonic humour, Clements had been secretly scouring the internet for alternative means of employment for some time now. He could have put together a sizeable file of evidence against his DCI for harassment, had he so chosen, but real men took it on the chin, didn't they – especially from a woman – even one as hardcore as Louise Lavache. Jack did not want to feel further emasculated than he did already, his life course steered by a dictatorial uncle and a witch in a trench coat.

The witch was devoid of the trench coat at that point in time, however. It was a beautiful Saturday morning in late spring, the first time temperatures had hit the twenties that year, and Louise Lavache was dressed simply in a black V-neck t-shirt and black skinny Levi's, as she marched back from the local convenience store in her size eight biker boots, bottle of Vimto and a bag of minty Aero Minis in her hand. Lavache had the sort of irritatingly fast metabolism that childless women in active jobs often had. A bordering on obsessive exercise routine and an aversion to alcohol enabled Lavache to put away the chocolate bars and sugary drinks without fear of physiological reprisal, much to the envy of several of her colleagues.

Lavache had plans that morning to drive to Newbury to pick up a rowing machine she had won on an online auction. She was just in the process of rearranging the seats in her car to accommodate the bulky item when the call came through from HQ.

"Boss, there's been a stabbing in Milton Welby. We need CID and SOCOS there."

"Milton Welby? Where the ferk is that?" Lavache barked, banging her head on the raised hatch of her 4x4 as she extricated herself from the back seats. She cursed loudly.

"For ferk sake," she grumbled, as the controller gave her the details. Not only a stabbing, but in a bloody church of all places. That brought together two of Lavache's pet hates:- places of worship and working on a weekend.

Who was least likely to be hungover? Lavache scrolled down and selected Clements' number. "Jake, get the team together, there's been a fatal stabbing in some poxy village off the A34 northbound – Melton Wilby. In the Utilitarian Church. Victim is female, late twenties, in a white dress and veil."

"It's Jack, boss. And I think you'll find it's Unitarian and Milton Welby."

"Whatever."

2

In the event, Sergeant Sienna Jones had arrived first at the scene of the crime, having been in the vicinity picking up some pet supplies from a local garden centre. As First Officer Attending, she had been responsible for sealing off the crime scene and assigning the local police to their tasks.

"What's the deal, then, Jones?" Lavache growled, slamming the door of her 4x4 *sans* rowing machine.

"Bride A of two found knifed in the back in the side chapel, boss."

"How very Christian," Lavache snarled, pushing past Jones and the uniformed officer guarding the entrance to the churchyard. "Didn't think the Church of England allowed lezzie weddings in any case."

"It's a Unitarian Church," Jones replied a tad smugly.

Lavache snorted. "Bloody taffs. Your lot know all about churches and choirs and all that religious crap."

"That's right, boss," Sienna commented sarcastically once Lavache was out of earshot. "That's all we do is sing and play rugby."

"What's her problem?" the PC in uniform asked.

"Internalised homophobia," Sienna grinned, and waved to Jack Clements and Gary Oakes who had arrived in Clements' modest Ford Fiesta.

"Good God!" Lavache whistled as she was confronted by the sight of an enormous white satin bedecked bottom on entering the side chapel.

"It appears the victim was stabbed in the back and fell forwards over the communion rail," Lavache was informed by the local uniformed police constable who had been guarding the crime scene until the DCI arrived.

"Looks that way, certainly," Lavache agreed. "SOCOs are on their way. Big girl!"

"Yes, Ma'am. Believe it or not, her name was Rotunda. Rotunda Wells."

Lavache nearly choked on the strong black coffee in her stainless-steel keep-cup. "Ferkin' hell, you're having a laugh!"

She slipped some plastic overshoes on and skirted around the white satin mound, doubled over the rail, taking care not to contaminate the scene. Blood trickled from a knife wound in the woman's back, whose heavily made-up face wore an expression of bog-eyed shock.

Hair like Miss Piggy, eyelashes like a cow, Lavache thought to herself. While there was nothing beautiful about the bride, she had certainly glammed herself up for her big day, sporting expensive diamante earrings and matching choker.

"No sign of the murder weapon?" Lavache asked the constable.

"Nope, though we haven't been able to do a search yet. All available manpower is being used to hold the wedding guests in the main church."

Lavache groaned. A church full of ferkin Christians and potentially queers to interview. Could her Saturday get any worse?

"Who discovered the body?"

"Her father," the young policeman replied.

Lavache whistled. "That'll be one walk down the aisle in a week's time he won't have been anticipating."

"Indeed, Ma'am," the constable nodded, thinking the remark was in rather poor taste.

"Where is he now? Obviously he's a suspect until proven otherwise."

"With the Serge in the church office," the constable replied. "He's in a hell of a state."

"I bet," Lavache muttered grimly. She surveyed the scene once more then left the room.

"DCI Louise Lavache, Hollingham CID," Lavache announced, barging tactlessly into the Milton Welby Unitarian Church Administrator's office.

A rather overstuffed middle-aged man in floods of tears sat hunched on the edge of a cheap plastic chair as Sergeant James Houlihan of Milton Welby Police stood up to greet his superior.

"I'll take over here," Lavache informed him, once introductions had been made. "Could you stay with the body until Scenes of Crime arrive?"

Houlihan gave her a frosty stare as the father of the bride let out a huge sob in response to the female detective's crass lack of tact.

Unabashed, Lavache discarded the plastic chair vacated by Houlihan and wheeled over a more comfortable chair from behind the administrator's desk. It did not occur to Lavache to offer the upholstered chair to the grief-stricken man as she wheeled it around him.

"As I understand it, it was you who discovered your daughter," she began, opening her notebook.

Sobbing, the red-faced fifty something nodded, twisting and untwisting a sodden handkerchief around his finger.

"Mr Wells, I believe?"

"Nigel. Nigel Wells," he sobbed. "Rotunda's my only daughter. Was…"

He burst into tears again. Lavache clicked in impatience. *Man up, for ferk's sake.* It was going to take some time to establish the facts at this rate. At least some more officers had arrived, Lavache noted through the window, as she waited for Wells to compose himself. It was going to be hell managing a church full of potential suspects.

It transpired that Rotunda and her father had been waiting in the side chapel. Rotunda's mother, Selina Wells, had refused to attend her only daughter's same-sex wedding – and that would certainly merit a thorough investigation. The plan had been that when Rotunda's bride, Phoebe, appeared at the back of the church to be escorted down the aisle by her father, the vicar Harvey Green, standing at the altar, would give the Church Warden the nod to knock on the door of the side chapel. Rotunda would then be escorted by Nigel along the side nave to the front of the church to meet her bride before the altar.

Shortly before the second bridal party was due to arrive at the church, however, there had been a howl of anguish from the side chapel, and an ashen-faced Nigel Wells had run out screaming into the main church, announcing to the shocked sixty strong congregation that his daughter had been murdered.

Nigel, it emerged, had left the side chapel just moments before to make a quick trip to the gents. In the two minutes that had elapsed, somebody had found their way into the side chapel and thrust a knife into the fleshy back of Rotunda Wells. For Nigel had returned to the chapel to find his daughter sprawled frontwards over the low-level gold altar rail, backside in the air, blood seeping from a wound just below the left shoulder blade.

Whilst the police were now busy questioning the wedding guests in the main church building, to ascertain whether anybody had seen a third party enter the side chapel, Nigel had certainly not seen anything suspicious. He confirmed that there were no other entrances to the side chapel. Whoever had murdered Rotunda had taken their chances discreetly and efficiently.

Lavache made some additional background notes then radioed for support. She needed to get among the wedding guests pronto, but Nigel Wells couldn't be left alone, though she doubted on this showing that he was a suspect. Someone must have seen something.

3

Gary Oakes had been assigned the unenviable task of interviewing the surviving bride, who had been diverted away from Milton Welby Unitarian Church in the bridal car by a quick thinking congregant and was currently sitting in the back room of the Welby Arms public house, flanked by her shocked parents.

Phoebe Toser was as skinny as Rotunda was chunky, Lavache noted, on entering the rather soulless back room of the local boozer. It stunk of bleach, having been recently cleaned. As Oakes had muttered in her ear on greeting her at the entrance, it was pretty clear who ate all the pies in this relationship, and it wasn't the wafer-thin Phoebe Toser.

Her parents, Jerry and Amelia, were equally malnourished in appearance, a state of affairs that was unlikely to improve over the next few months, Lavache thought. They looked totally numb.

Phoebe and her parents had pulled up outside the church at two minutes to eleven, in a white Jaguar bedecked with bridal ribbons driven by Phoebe's paternal uncle, Andrew Toser.

But before mother and bride had emerged from the back of the Jag, one of the ushers had run out, face aghast. At that point, they had not been informed of the awful truth, but simply told that there had been an accident at the church and the building was cordoned off. That thankless task had been left to Gary Oakes.

"I'm sorry, but I will need to ask you lots of questions," Lavache began. "For one, I can't read my sergeant's handwriting, and secondly, I need to establish your precise movements this morning."

The parents nodded disconsolately as their daughter rocked miserably back and fore on the wooden bench on which the three were uncomfortably perched.

Phoebe, Jerry and Amelia Toser had left their house just two streets away in the bridal car minutes before pulling up outside the church. That morning had started with a large breakfast at eight am, aimed at staving off the hunger pangs until the inevitable delayed wedding meal booked for 3pm at a local hotel in neighbouring Shipton Welby.

A mobile hairdresser and beautician had then arrived to touch up mother and daughter's hair, which had been styled the day before, prior to the family dressing for the wedding. Nobody had left the house and several neighbours who had been washing their cars or tending to their front gardens could vouch for that.

From what Lavache could gather, there was no reason to suspect either of the parents bore their future daughter-in-law any ill will. They appeared to be accepting of both their daughter's sexual orientation and choice of partner. Whilst they acknowledged there had been difficulties with

Rotunda's mother refusing to engage with the forthcoming nuptials, they did not believe Selina Wells would have committed such a heinous crime.

"She's a dyed in the wool, Daily Mail reading Conservative," Jerry Toser remarked, "But kill her own daughter? No way."

"No mother would ever do that," Amelia concurred, shaking her head definitively.

"You'd be surprised," Lavache replied darkly. She slapped her notebook shut. "Ok, you're free to go home now. We may need to ask more questions but that's all for today. And – erm – I'm very sorry for your loss."

Lavache, who patently didn't give a monkey's, turned on her heel and left the room.

❀❀❀❀

Lavache elected to return to the church on foot, glad for some fresh air after the chemical overload of the freshly scrubbed down pub function room.

"Got anything?" she enquired of Jack Clements, arriving back in the main church worship area, where half a dozen police officers were questioning the assorted wedding guests, the linked church seating separated out now. Little groupings of witnesses and police were dotted around the main hall in small groups.

"Nope, nobody so far has seen a thing," Clements replied. "You can't see the chapel door from the main church hall, it's further down the corridor. But various people nipped out to the loo before the service was due to start, and nobody so far has seen anything."

Lavache frowned. "But it's possible one of them murdered the fat lass while her dad nipped to the bog?"

Clements shook his head again. "The Minister, Harvey Green, said nobody left the room in the five minutes or so before Nigel Wells ran into the church. Green was standing at the altar watching for signs of the bride arriving at the main doors, so he had a bird's eye view of the whole congregation. And we know Nigel ran into the room at about five to eleven, just minutes before the second bridal car arrived outside. There was only just time for one of the ushers to run outside and divert the car."

"And there's definitely no way of getting into the side chapel apart from the main door to the church?"

"Nope. The only window in the chapel is a big, old-fashioned, stained glass leaded window which doesn't open at all."

"And the vicar's telling the truth – about not seeing anyone?"

"He's a man of God, boss," Jack grinned, knowing full well what response that would evoke.

Lavache snorted obligingly and made a note to check in with the wardens about Green's eyesight, as well as his integrity.

"Nice of Kaur to turn up," she remarked darkly, noting the young Detective Constable enter the room, head down, looking slightly the worse for wear that Saturday lunchtime. But there wasn't time to give her a bollocking at this point in time; it could wait until Monday morning. There were more pressing matters to attend to.

Lavache scoured the room and spotted her desired target. She marched purposefully across the room to the far corner, where the upright figure of the Reverend Harvey Green could be seen, sipping strong tea from a standard church issue olive coloured bone china cup.

"Reverend Green? Detective Chief Inspector Louise Lavache, Hollingham CID. I'm the Senior Investigating Officer here."

The vicar put his cup down on the tiled window sill and extended a rather damp hand.

Lavache shook it distastefully. Was he nervous? He didn't look it, but his clammy palm suggested otherwise.

"A thoroughly dreadful business. Sort of thing you see on television, not in real life."

"Indeed," Lavache concurred. "All very *Midsomer Murders*. Not your run of the mill domestic – at least not on first appearances."

The vicar narrowed his eyes. "You don't think it could involve one of the family, do you?"

"Unless the bride of the mother got in through the keyhole or Dad deserves an Oscar, then no, doesn't look like it."

"Hmm," Green responded, frowning at the flippancy of the young DCI. Was he getting old, or was everyone younger in post these days? Professional people did seem to lack a certain gravitas these days, Green thought, and this rather butch looking Detective Chief Inspector in her jeans and clumpy boots was no exception.

"Do you mind if I ask you some questions, Vicar?" Lavache enquired, making it abundantly clear he had little choice in the matter, as she poured herself a tea from the makeshift refreshments table set up and pulled up a chair.

"I'm a minister, actually," Green corrected her, resignedly taking a seat opposite the tall, black-haired DCI. "This is a Unitarian Church, not C of E."

"Pardon me, not too up on religious stuff," Lavache apologised unapologetically. "It looks pretty much like every other church I've ever been in. Not that there's been many."

"No, I don't expect there have been," Green replied dryly. "It was an Anglican Church until eight years ago," he continued. "But the congregation died out and the local diocese decided it wasn't viable anymore as a place of worship. The Unitarian Church rent out the building from the Diocese, so technically it is still an Anglican Church, but we are the only congregation that worships here."

"And how many come here?" Lavache enquired, making notes.

"Around fifty or so," Green responded. "And we have a growing number of young families."

"Really?" Lavache looked up, unable to disguise her surprise.

"You know it's a common misconception that young people lack spirituality, Detective Chief Inspector," the minister informed her tartly. "They've simply been put off by outmoded and ill-informed church teaching that has nothing to do with the central ethos of the Scriptures and other sacred writings. The Unitarian Church is open to all, people of all creeds and colours, genders and sexual orientations."

Spare me the Equality and Diversity spiel, Lavache groaned inwardly. "So that's why you're able to perform same sex weddings? The Utilit… Unitarian Church allows it?"

"Yes, I'm pleased to say we do not discriminate against anyone who seeks to formalise a loving and mutually beneficial relationship, such as the relationship between Phoebe and Rotunda."

His voice tailed off and he took another sip of the strong tea.

Lavache considered the sixty something church leader as he confirmed that he had seen nobody leave the main church hall during the relevant window of opportunity. Whilst he couldn't be far off retirement, there was nothing remotely doddery about Harvey Green and neither was there anything to suggest he was anything other than a person of his word. What age did clergy retire, anyway? Some of them looked positively ancient, in Lavache's experience, which was based mainly on TV caricatures rather than actual real life clerics.

"How well did you know the deceased?" Lavache enquired.

"Not very well at all, to be honest," Green replied, shaking his head. "The Wells family live in Hollingham and aren't regular churchgoers, to the best of my knowledge. I know Phoebe's parents. Jerry and Amelia attend fairly regularly and it's through them that Phoebe had inquired about holding the wedding here at St Mary's."

"Don't you hold wedding classes or something beforehand?" Lavache frowned. "Or is that just an old- fashioned things these days?"

"Not at all," Green replied. "We do indeed run marriage preparation classes, but my Associate Minister met with Phoebe and Rotunda."

"Oh yes?" Lavache pricked up her ears. This was the first mention of another leader at the church.

"Karen knew both of them quite well, I should think," Green continued. "They'd had three or four meetings, on a Tuesday evening. They could only do a Tuesday because of various work commitments, but that's the one night I couldn't do. I won't bore you with the details of the Buildings Committee –"

No, please don't, Lavache thought to herself.

"But I chair those meetings, so Karen stepped in."

"Karen?"

"Dervish," Green replied.

Lavache made a note. "And Karen Dervish isn't here today?" She looked up and met Green's pale blue eyes.

He shook his head. "No, she had a prior engagement."

"Is she licensed to er…"

"Officiate at weddings?" Green obliged, seeing the DCI was clearly out of her comfort zone. "Yes, she is."

Lavache frowned. "Rather odd, isn't it, that she wasn't at least here, if not err… officiating at the wedding? I mean, she must have built up quite a relationship with them? I guess you talk about some pretty private stuff in such classes?"

"I was a little surprised that Karen made herself unavailable, I must admit," Green replied.

"Made herself unavailable – what do you mean?" Lavache's ears pricked up again.

"Well, Karen was on the rota originally for today, but then told me a few weeks ago that she needed to visit her elderly aunt and would I mind swapping with her? I was free, so agreed to it."

"Hmm. A bit odd, don't you think?"

Green considered it. "She *is* very devoted to her aunt, and her aunt is quite a formidable woman. So it's just possible she might have kicked off if Karen had tried to put her off to another day. Lottie is quite fierce, as I remember. I've only met her once or twice, though."

"Do you know where this aunt lives?"

"Yes, in Shipton Welby, the bungalows that run along the street behind the primary school. Number seven. Her name's Widdecombe, Lottie Widdecombe. Used to attend St Mary's when it was still Anglican. But her eyesight is pretty bad these days, by all accounts. But not lost her faculties or anything like that. Certainly not. I suspect she doesn't get out much at all – and she wouldn't set foot in a Unitarian Church in any case. She would see that as beyond the pale, I should imagine."

Green made a despairing face.

"All that denominational stuff is lost on me, I'm afraid, Reverend," Lavache smiled thinly. She slapped her notebook shut and stood up. "Excuse me a moment er... Minister."

Lavache walked across to Clements and took him to one side.

"Jake – get yourself over to the next village, Shipton something. Check out whether the vicar's sidekick, a Karen Dervish, is visiting some old biddy at bungalow number seven behind the primary school. And let me know the moment you find out anything."

Jack nodded, glad to escape the creepy old church building with its smell of old hymn books.

Lavache marched over to Mandeep Kaur, who was sipping black coffee and attempting to stay awake as she took statements from wedding guests in the far corner. The young woman looked utterly bored.

"Kaur," Lavache began, once the interviewees were dismissed. "Make yourself useful now you're finally here. I need you to dig some dirt on the Minister and his sidekick. Both seem too ferkin' good to be true. Root out the church gossips and get me some back story."

Mandeep nodded wearily and took a larger slurp of her Americano.

4

"Ok, sit down and shut up," Lavache commanded at 9 a.m. that Monday morning in the incident room of Hollingham CID.

She indicated to the board, where a series of unflattering shots of Rotunda's rear view were attached alongside a map of the church layout.

"We know that Rotunda Wells was stabbed in the back with a large knife – possibly a chef's knife - in the side chapel of St Mary's Church, Milton Welby, at approximately 10.50 am on Saturday. The knife entered her back on the left-hand side just below her shoulder blade and pierced her heart. Death would have been instantaneous. Her body was discovered by her father, Nigel Wells, who had briefly left the room to use the Gents further down the corridor. Father and daughter were waiting in the chapel until her partner arrived – it had all been choregraphed in advance – so that the two brides met at the altar, with Phoebe being accompanied up the aisle from the back door of the church by her father, Jerry, and Rotunda being walked up the side aisle by Nigel."

Lavache paused for breath. "The Minister, Harvey Green, who was taking the service, was stood at the altar and had a full view of the church, including the front doors. He assures us that no guests left the room in the five minutes preceding the point at which Nigel entered the main hall screaming that his daughter had been murdered."

"How do we know Nigel went to the bog when he said he did?" Gary Oakes enquired. "He could have been mistaken… it could have been earlier, and one of the people who were spotted going to the loo earlier by the vicar nipped in and killed the bride, while Nigel was taking a piss."

"Eloquent as always," Lavache commented, giving him a derisory look. "Green saw him walk down the corridor to the loo at the time he said he did. You can see a bit of the corridor, but not the chapel door, through some open stalls in the main church hall. The side chapel and toilets are situated along the corridor to the right of the main church worship area, from where Green was standing."

"Well, Nigel must have done it, then," Oakes shrugged. "There's no other explanation, if nobody saw anyone leave the worship area or enter the front door, and there's no other entrance to the chapel."

"Greasy, this is a man who named his daughter after a word he saw on an Ordnance Survey map because it sounded like a nice word! He's not the sharpest knife in the drawer."

Clements winced at the unfortunate pun.

"Well, she certainly grew into her name!" Sienna cackled. Lavache glared at her. It wasn't as if Sienna wasn't carrying some extra timber herself.

"Exactly," Gary slapped the table. "Thick as shit. Had to be him."

"So, Greasy, what's his motive, then?" Lavache enquired impatiently.

Oakes shrugged.

There was silence.

"The way I see it," Lavache continued, "there are three possibilities. Either the Minister missed somebody slip out, or there was someone hanging around further down the corridor out of sight that Green didn't spot slip into the chapel, or Green himself is lying to protect the killer. Kaur – did you get anything on the Minister?"

Kaur shook her head. "Nobody had a bad word to say about him. Seems to be totally respected by all, and his back story checks out."

"Jake – what about his sidekick, Karen?"

Jack opened his notebook. "Karen Dervish was at the property when I arrived at 13.07 on Saturday afternoon. Her aunt, who was pretty doddery, admittedly, but had all her marbles, confirmed that Karen had arrived at ten thirty with some food shopping and had been with her all morning. They were eating lunch when I got there."

"What's she like, this Karen Dervish?" Lavache enquired.

Clements shrugged. "Nothing special. Medium height, long blondish grey hair, chunky without being fat, big glasses."

"I mean her character, Jake, not her ferkin' sex appeal," Lavache snorted.

You sure about that? Sienna snickered in Gary's ear. He chuckled and Lavache glared at him.

"Uninspiring, harmless, I'd say," Clements shrugged.

"So, basically she's in the clear?" Lavache surmised.

Clements nodded. "It would seem so, boss."

Lavache turned her attention to Sienna Jones.

"Jones, you were checking out the no-show homophobic mother for me."

Sienna nodded. "Selina Wells spent the morning shopping in Hollingham and met a friend for lunch in Marks and Spencers at noon. The friend, a Louise Arnott, confirmed this was true and they were spotted by the restaurant supervisor at that time, too."

"But we have no alibi prior to twelve noon?" Lavache frowned.

"We have an officer checking the CCTV for Hollingham town centre, but it's slow going, as you might imagine," Jones replied.

"She could have got from the church to Hollingham by twelve though," Lavache commented. "Assuming she drove there."

"She did drive, boss," Jones confirmed. "But we have no sightings of her anywhere in the church building and it's unlikely, from what she told me, that she would want to set foot in the place on the day of her daughter's lesbian wedding. She was vehemently against the relationship."

"But more to the point, who would want to kill their own daughter?" Clements frowned.

Kaur snorted. "My mother would kill me if I took a lesbian partner, I can tell you that now."

"We can't rule anything out," Lavache stated. "And homophobia may not be the only reason Selina Wells didn't want to attend her daughter's wedding. Did you dig anything else up, Sienna?"

"I couldn't get anything else out of her," Jones replied. "She wasn't crying her eyes out like the father, but she was clearly very shocked and didn't want to speak ill of her daughter. She admitted she didn't approve of the wedding on religious grounds and had made it clear to the girls that she would not be attending, but more than that, she didn't say. She was very difficult to read, to be honest. But then not everyone bares their soul in public, do they?" She gave her boss a pointed look.

Lavache ignored her. She had no intention of squawking about her personal life in public as Sienna was prone to doing. It was neither cool nor clever, in her carefully maintained book.

"The fact remains, though," Gary continued, "that unless the vicar is lying or took his eyes off the ball temporarily, there's no way anyone could have got into that side chapel and stabbed Rotunda Wells, apart from her father."

"Logically, I would have to agree. However, the direction of travel of the stab wound tells us the murderer was right-handed, and Nigel Wells is a leftie."

"How do you know that?" Oakes frowned, who would not be thwarted.

"Because he was holding a mug of tea in his left hand when Sienna called around the house yesterday to speak to Selina Wells. I got her to check. It's in Sienna's very detailed and legible notes, Greasy," Lavache added sarcastically for good measure. Jones grinned at Oakes and nodded in confirmation. Oakes made a slurping noise at her to indicate she was a suck-up.

"What about the church itself – does that have CCTV?" Kaur asked.

Sienna Jones laughed. "You've got to be joking! CCTV in Milton Welby? This is the first serious crime the local plod has attended in donkey's years! They were bloody clueless when I got there."

"Sadly not," Lavache confirmed. "Do we have any news back on the murder weapon, Kaur?"

Kaur shook her head. "It's still not been found. We've established it's a chef's knife and we've been ringing around retail outlets, trying to trace local purchasers. However, it's likely been in somebody's drawer for years, or it was purchased online and we have a cat's chance in hell of tracing it."

"Not your average flick-knife then?"

Kaur shook her head.

"Clements – what about the door to door enquiries?"

"Nobody saw anyone untoward hanging around outside the church," Jack replied. "Just wedding guests from about 10.15 onwards. Bagging the best seats, I guess. There were a few tradesmen seen in white vans delivering parcels – delivery drivers and the like – around the village, and the brewery truck pulled up at the pub about ten am, but nobody was spotted in the church grounds – apart from the Sockman."

"The Sockman? Who the ferk is he?" Lavache queried, frowning in befuddlement.

"Local character, boss," Clements replied. "Has what we'd term learning differences these days."

Lavache snorted.

"He walks miles every day filling a bag with random items of clothing he finds discarded, then takes them to the cash for clothing place in Nolton."

Nolton Welby was the third and largest in the triangle of Welby villages alongside Milton and Shipton. Lavache and Kaur wrinkled their noses up in disdain.

"And does he have a name, this *Sockman*?" Lavache enquired sarcastically.

"Nobody knows, but he shouldn't be too difficult to track down."

"I want him interviewed," Lavache barked. "I need a name. He might have a record – I want him checked out."

"A record for what? Stealing washing off the line?" Gary Oakes guffawed at his own joke. Lavache glared at him before returning to Clements.

"And what about inside the church?"

"I've scoured through all the witness statements, as requested, and none of the wedding guests saw anyone who wasn't a guest, a church warden, or Harvey Green in the church building. The ushers confirmed that no gate-crashers, so to speak, were spotted outside or inside the church building, and all guests present were on the official list."

"Who opened the church?"

"The Minister himself at ten a.m.," Clements replied. "Then the warden arrived."

"No florists or any other external visitors to the church?" Lavache checked.

Clements shook his head. "The flowers in the church were done by Rotunda and her bridesmaids the night before. They organised it themselves – to save money, I guess."

"No journos sniffing around for some salacious pics?"

"Nope."

"Well, ferk me," Lavache sighed. "I think David Blane pulled this one off."

"It certainly looks that way, boss," Jack Clements concurred.

5

One of Louise Lavache's main strengths, alongside physical agility, was a hardness of heart that protected her from the emotional burnout that befell many of her more humane colleagues. Lavache was able to compartmentalise her work, switching off entirely from the often grisly events of the day the moment she walked through the front door.

But the conundrum of Rotunda Wells' fatal stabbing just refused to exit her thoughts as she pounded the treadmill in her home gym that evening. The murder enquiry had absorbed all her free time since Saturday morning, so the purchased rowing machine still sat waiting at the seller's house in Newbury. Fortunately, the vendor had been very understanding; after all, it wasn't everyday your purchaser didn't show up because they were leading a murder enquiry. Lavache had already graced *South Today* several times, as well as BBC News 24 and Sky News, so there was no querying that particular excuse.

Lavache was convinced Nigel Wells had not stabbed his own daughter. He was patently distraught at Rotunda's murder and it did not appear to Lavache to be guilt-ridden grief. Besides, there was absolutely no motive whatsoever on his part. He clearly adored his daughter. Selina Wells, on the other hand, was a cold fish, who appeared to harbour no particular warmth towards her own offspring. Yet neither did she appear sufficiently hate-fuelled to have committed filicide. And while she technically had the opportunity until CCTV footage proved otherwise, she had not been seen in the building.

Phoebe Toser's family were entirely ruled out, and again, had absolutely no reason to want Rotunda dead. Jerry and Amelia Toser were clearly very fond of their prospective daughter-in-law and Phoebe was absolutely devoted to her fiancée.

Lavache had herself tried to rattle some skeletons in her interview with Phoebe the previous day, but to no avail. There were no jilted lovers, or bitter bunny-boilers in either of their lives and Phoebe was at a total loss as to who might have wished her good-natured, well-liked partner dead.

Lavache sighed. There was nothing for it but to stay up into the early hours poring through the statements once more. The Chief Constable had called a press briefing for the following morning, as the grisly murder in a picturesque English village had made headlines both nationally and further afield. The press was having a field day, with the local rag coming up with the headline, *Reverend Green in the Chapel with the Dagger*. They could have a serious libel case on their hands, if they weren't careful, though Harvey Green didn't strike Lavache as the kind of man to let a silly tabloid headline throw him off course.

Police blockades had already been set up on all roads leading into the village, much to the relief of local residents, who had been subjected to a barrage of press intrusion when the story had first leaked – undoubtedly from the social media account of one of the wedding guests, Lavache was sure. Bloody kids these days. They couldn't keep their traps shut about anything. You couldn't ferkin' breathe without somebody posting it on at least ten different social media platforms. Some people seriously needed to get a life, she thought, debating which Netflix boxset to put on later while she sifted through the interview transcripts.

❀❀❀❀

An hour and a half later, Lavache sat on the sofa, feet up on the coffee table, a Scandi crime drama playing out as she embarked upon her reading project for the evening. But it was no use. She couldn't focus on subtitled Swedish drama *and* give her full attention to the transcripts. She flicked the TV off and put on a Melissa Etheridge album in the background instead. She'd never heard of the Emmy winning American songstress until recently, when her one and only ex-college friend had recommended the artist. Lavache found herself enjoying the rousing guitars and rasping vocals.

Meh meh meh… Oakes and Kaur really did need some training on the art of interviews and note taking.

37

These were appalling. She scoured through them, but they revealed diddly squat. She sighed in relief as she came to Clements' reports. That lad might look like a ferkin' twelve year old and have that twat Neville Clements as his uncle, but she couldn't deny he was a details man, which was precisely what she needed on a team with Greasy Oik and Slapdash Kaur on board.

Lavache skimmed the first few lines of a statement from Clements before sitting up straighter. This was more interesting. The church warden, Nadine Trot, had done a bit of a number on the Associate Minister, Karen Dervish. Odd that Clements hadn't mentioned it at the briefing in the incident room earlier, but then it didn't place Dervish in the building, so maybe he'd deemed it insignificant.

"Nadine stated that Karen Dervish was very ambitious and thought it odd that she hadn't officiated at the same sex wedding. The event was causing a bit of a ripple among the local villagers, who weren't happy that their old church was being used for a lesbian wedding. Dervish had written a few letters to the local paper in response to indignant former parishioners, supporting the relationship and the use of the church for their marriage. Karen seemed to be like being in the limelight and Nadine expressed surprise that she hadn't wanted to officiate and grab the headlines. The witness felt that Karen had her eye on Harvey Green's job and beyond."

Ouch! Lavache grinned. It was interesting, but Dervish had an alibi and wouldn't be the first to harbour ambition in the workplace. Lavache felt Sienna Jones snapping at her ankles; the Oik knew he wasn't DCI material. Still, the angry ex-parishioners bit was potentially significant. Lavache made a note to chastise Clements for not mentioning this at their briefing, even though as Senior Investigating Officer, she ought to have reread the statements herself by now. Lavache's Blame Apportionment Strategy rarely if ever included herself. She would get Clements to track down the newspaper letters and perhaps reinterview Trot or Dervish.

She doublechecked Clements' report on the visit to Lottie Widdecombe in Shipton Welby, but it all stacked up. Clements had even noted the contents of their lunch and the fact that Widdecombe had exceedingly posh crockery! That figured, if the old biddie lived in Shipton, by far the most exclusive of the Welby triad of villages.

Lavache skimmed through the rest of the reports, but there was nothing of note. The Sockman still hadn't been traced and neither had the source of the murder weapon or the murder weapon itself. CCTV footage from the multi-story carpark in Hollingham had captured a stony-faced Selina Wells purchasing a ticket from the Pay and Display machine at 11.13 a.m. on Saturday morning, thereby absolving her of the murder, as it was a good half hour drive to

Hollingham from Milton Welby on a busy Saturday morning.

She grimaced. It was going to be hard to placate the Chief Constable in the morning.

6

Fresh from an early morning bollocking from the witch for not thoroughly disclosing information from the witness statements, Jack Clements decided to step his efforts up a notch and get back on Lavache's less than evil side (for there was no good side). He was scared of what she might say to the Chief Constable, who was exceedingly pally with his Uncle Neville. Such thoughts fuelled his decision to drive the twelve-mile distance to Milton Welby. It was a nice day and perhaps the Sockman would be out and about, filling his plastic sack with discarded weekend underpants and random unpaired shoes.

Flashing his warrant card at the uniformed officers guarding the entrance to the village, he parked his Fiesta in the church carpark. It now lay desolate, having been packed on Saturday with an assortment of squad cars and vehicles belonging to the wedding guests. He tried the church door, but it was locked. Course it was.

Clements walked through a modest graveyard to the side of the church building. He followed the steeple upwards with his eyes. Despite its relatively small footprint, it was an imposing building – late Norman, Clements thought. The roof looked in good condition, which he knew was unusual for most church buildings these days. Perhaps the Unitarian Church had paid for its upkeep; it was unlikely the

Diocese would fork out, now it was no longer a site of Anglican worship.

"Ow!" Clements exclaimed, as he suddenly tripped and had to grab an overhanging branch to keep his balance. He looked down at a jutting out piece of concrete on a crumbling grave. He kicked it back into place and rubbed the dirt off his shoe with a leaf from the overhanging tree branch. Someone should report that before an elderly or infirm person came a cropper.

Purchasing a milky tea with three sugars from the local coffee shop, Clements made a tour of the village. But the Sockman was nowhere to be seen. Clements sighed, feeling hot and clammy in his grey suit in the May sunshine. He returned to his car to make the short trip to Shipton Welby. The tie and suit jacket would have to go.

❀❀❀❀

In the end, Lavache had got off lightly. The Chief Constable, eager to suppress the scurrilous headlines surrounding the so-called 'Lesbian Wedding Murder,' had praised Hollingham CID to the hilt for their dogged attempts thus-far to bring the perpetrator to justice. (He had attempted to correct the journalist with 'same sex wedding murder' on numerous occasions, but the technicality was lost on them and besides, it didn't make for such salacious headlines). Lavache suspected Neville Clements had been singing young Jack's praises to his great golfing buddy and for once, Lavache was glad to have the former DCI's nephew on the team – not that she was going to admit that to Jack.

Lavache checked out her appearance in the mirror of the Ladies at Hollingham CID. Yep, she was looking good, suited and booted in black with her dark eyebrows neatly shaped. She knew she would be all over the local news tonight, having taken questions from journalists alongside the Chief Constable, in her capacity as SIO on the case.

Lavache grabbed her car keys. Time to pay a visit to Reverend Green, but this time in his home, and hopefully minus a dagger.

❀❀❀❀

"A phone-call first might have been courteous," Harvey Green frowned, opening the door to Lavache twenty minutes later from his home on the far side of Hollingham.

"Is it a bad time, then?" Lavache enquired, her tone of voice conveying that she cared little whether it was or not. It was always best to catch potential accessories or perpetrators unawares, in her experience.

"Kind of," Green replied, gesticulating in frustration with his hands as he led her through to a sizeable study at the back of the spacious detached property. Did the Utilitarian Church or whatever it was called pay for this, Lavache wondered.

"Fer- lip," Lavache caught herself just in time. "Having some work done on the house?"

Green had architects' plans spread out over his desk.

"No no, it's for the church. They just arrived, actually. I was just about to take a look at them." It was a pointed comment.

"Ah, the Buildings Committee?" Lavache enquired.

"Indeed," the Minister confirmed. "Tea or coffee, DCI?"

"Just an iced water would be good, thanks. It's hotter than you think out there today."

Especially if you dress all in black like an undertaker, Harvey Green thought to himself, making his way to the kitchen. He liked women to look feminine and not dress like SS guards.

Lavache wasted no time in availing herself of the 'open access' information in Green's study, once he had left the room. She gave the plans a cursory glance before turning to his computer. From an open email, it looked like the Unitarian Church had agreed to pay the lion's share of the renovations to the building. Lavache scrolled down the email chain and read. She pulled out her phone and took some quick snapshots.

"Don't you require a warrant for that? Green asked coldly, re-entering the room with a glass of iced water in his hand.

"Technically," Lavache replied. "But then you've nothing to worry about if you've nothing to hide."

She grinned somewhat malevolently at him and took a chair the right side of the desk.

"I'm not sure that's quite the point, DCI Lavache," Green said archly.

He folded the plans up and locked his computer screen. "So, what can I do for you?"

"Let's start with the anti-lezzie brigade, shall we?" Lavache smirked and took a sip of her water.

Green sighed. It was not the productive afternoon he had planned. This foul woman with her snarky insinuations was sure to leave a nasty taste in his mouth.

7

Lavache surveyed the team in the Incident Room at just after 9 a.m. on Wednesday morning. It had been four days and they were still no closer to catching the killer of Rotunda Wells.

The investigation was irrevocably stuck. It appeared that the invisible right-handed man had murdered Rotunda Wells. The pathologist had all but ruled out a woman, given the physical strength required to thrust a large chef's knife with force through Rotunda's fleshy back and out the other side. If it was a woman, it would need to be someone with considerable strength and dexterity – a woman who worked out, perhaps, who had a grievance against Rotunda or lesbians in general. In fact, someone just like the DCI, the pathologist had thought, but dared not verbalise.

"Any joy with our resident halfwit?" Lavache asked heartlessly.

"The Sockman has disappeared into thin air," Clements replied. "I've done several reckies of the area, questioned the locals but nobody's seen hide nor hair of him since Saturday morning. As I said last time, he was seen ambling around the village on Saturday morning but nowhere near the front of the church and one of the church regulars, who was also a wedding guest, confirmed that he wasn't allowed inside the church for … er… safeguarding reasons."

"Bloody snobs!" Sienna exclaimed. "Didn't Jesus welcome the riff raff in?"

"Jesus isn't in Milton Welby," Lavache informed her curtly, closing down the God talk at the earliest possible opportunity. "I know we've covered this already, but just humour me – there was no other entrance to the church open on Saturday, was there?"

Sienna Jones shook her head. "No, boss. I can confirm that the fire doors at the back of the church were locked from the inside and there are no side entrances. The only way in was from the main front door that leads into the foyer of the church outside the main hall where the wedding took place. From the main foyer, a corridor runs right down to the church office and vestry and to the left leading down to the side chapel and Ladies and Gents toilets."

Lavache slapped the table in frustration. "I just don't ferkin' get it."

There was a pause while Lavache collected her thoughts.

"Ok, Greasy and Jones. I want you both scouring the area for the Sockman."

"With respect, boss, while he's apparently quite a big guy, I don't think he has the nous for murder, by the sounds of it," Clements frowned, feeling slighted by his superior, who evidently didn't rate his efforts to locate the one man clothes bank the previous day.

"I agree, Jake," Lavache replied, "but he might have seen someone if he was sniffing around the area. We've got statements from all the wedding guests and neighbours – he's the only person we haven't spoken to."

"What can I do, boss?" Mandeep Kaur piped up.

"That's a very good question, Kaur. What *can* you do?" And with a sarcastic flourish, Lavache left the room.

❁❁❁❁

There was something troubling Jack Clements. Lavache had mentioned something during the briefing about a church buildings project. But as far as he could see, the church was in pretty good nick. The roof had obviously been repaired fairly recently and the inside of the church, though uninspiring, was perfectly functional. True, it could do with a lick of paint and some USB charging points in the pews, but with a congregation of fifty to sixty each week and just a smattering of children, Clements was struggling to see why a buildings committee was required.

Should he risk the wrath of Lavache this morning? She was not in the best of moods, given the utter lack of progress on the case. The press had her spiteful little head on the block. But he'd already had a dressing down once that week for withholding potentially useful information, so there was only one thing for it. He knocked on the DCI's door.

Lavache barked at him to enter, and he felt a blush rise up his neck and face as he stood before her desk. She really was terrifying, with her angular facial features and jet-black hair, close cropped apart from a quiff that fell over her left eye. She was a hybrid of Lisbeth Salander and Saga Noren, Clements thought, who was into his Scandi noir. (In actual fact, she was a dead ringer for an early KD Lang, a fact of which the young Clements was blissfully unaware). Lisbeth for the black hair, Saga for the long coat and bloody rudeness – a Saga Salander. At least Saga Noren was on the spectrum. Lavache had no such excuse. She was just a nasty bitch, period.

"What is it then, Jake?" she frowned, scrolling down an arsy email from the Chief Constable, whose patience was now wearing thin, given the adverse newspaper headlines.

"Boss, there's something bothering me," he replied.

"Do I look like an agony aunt?" Lavache complained, still reading. When Clements did not reply, she turned finally to face him.

Jack took a deep breath. "It's this buildings committee thing."

"What about it?" Lavache whipped back impatiently.

"Well, why are they having weekly meetings about renovating the church? It looks in pretty good condition and they're hardly bursting at the seams, numbers wise. I mean, it just feels rather odd."

"Go on," Lavache encouraged him, her internal antennae beginning to fizzle.

"It just doesn't make sense, that's all. I had a scout about the outside of the building yesterday – I couldn't get inside; it was still locked for Forensics to finish their investigations – and the roof is in great condition, looks like it's been done fairly recently. Plus, there were no signs of rotting masonry or other major repairs needed. The only thing I spotted was a broken grave, when I nearly went arse over tit over some fallen concrete."

"Hmm." Lavache paused for a moment then in a moment of snap decision, picked up the phone handset. "Get me Forensics, please."

8

"So, what's the plan, boss?" Clements asked as he scuttled in the wake of Lavache, who was striding across the station carpark towards her 4x4.

"We're meeting Green at the church, he's going to let us in," Lavache replied tersely, bleeping her car unlocked. Fortunately, the post school-run roads were relatively quiet and the two CID officers arrived at Milton Welby within twenty minutes.

There was a modest Honda Jazz in the church carpark – Harvey Green's, Lavache presumed. Trust a vicar to own a granny-mobile, she thought sarcastically. Lavache was a car snob and ageist, with it.

She turned the iron ring knocker to the ancient church door. It was open. Lavache called out to the Minister, but there was no response. Her voice echoed in the stone floored foyer.

"Odd," Lavache frowned.

"Perhaps he's in one of the side rooms and didn't hear us," Clements ventured. "He could have headphones on."

"What, listening to Spotify or something?" Lavache scoffed.

Clements shrugged. It had only been an idea. They walked into the main church worship area, but there was no sign of Green. The side chapel where Rotunda Wells had met her savage fate was locked. Clements knocked tentatively at the door of the gents but there was no response. Pushing him to one side, Lavache marched into the opposite sex toilet facilities but Green was not there.

"Church office," Lavache grunted and they returned to the foyer to take the opposite side corridor that led to the administrator's room where she'd first interviewed the grieving Nigel Wells.

"It's open," Lavache noted, trying the handle. It didn't take them long to locate their target. The Reverend Harvey Green was sprawled across the desk in a pool of blood, eyes wide open in shock, his grey marl sweater stained dark red from a knife wound to the back.

Lavache took the Lord's name in vain as she tentatively walked around the blood dripping on the floor to the front of the desk.

Clements felt sick. He hadn't actually seen Rotunda Wells' body in the side chapel and this was the first time he'd come up close and personal with a live murder scene.

"Shall I put the call out, boss?" he asked, somewhat shakily.

"Just give it a moment, I want to do a few investigations of my own before the overalls come in and boot us out."

Clements watched as Lavache peered closely at the vicar's face.

"What are you looking for, boss? I mean, he's obviously been stabbed like Rotunda."

Lavache pulled some latex gloves out of her pocket and slipped them on. Clements watched aghast as she gently prized Green's forehead off the table and extracted a tiny slip of paper.

"What are you doing? Shouldn't you...."

"I'll bag the evidence, don't you worry, Jake," Lavache replied. She put the slip of cream coloured paper in a small evidence bag she also carried a permanent supply of in her jacket pocket. She held the clear bag up to Jack. "See what this is?"

"Not really boss. Some kind of map?"

"Plans, Jake – architect's drawings. Remember what I said Green was doing when I paid him a visit the other day?"

"Looking at plans for the church," Clements replied, enlightened.

"So, he's looking at plans, while he waits for us, and the murderer comes into the room behind him – the desk's facing away towards the window – and stabs him in the back. They want the plans, but they're weighed down by his head that has fallen forward over them. So, they snatch at them – probably in the rush to make a getaway – and a small corner is trapped under his forehead, which serves as a paperweight."

Clements puffed his cheeks out at Lavache's summary of events.

"Stay here and ring the team, I'm going outside to take a recky," Lavache commanded. "This must have happened since we rang him, the murderer might still be in the area. When you've made the call, double-check there's nobody hiding anywhere inside."

"But we only rang him an hour ago," Clements frowned – how did he get to the church so quickly?"

"He took the call from here," Lavache replied. "He was already in the building, said he had work to catch up on, now that Forensics had given him the all clear to return."

Lavache headed straight for the churchyard. Something Clements had said earlier had got her cogs whirring.

She saw a couple of elderly villagers across the road nudge each other as they spotted her outside the church. *Give them something to gossip about*, Lavache thought grimly. Well, they'd have plenty to talk about in fifteen minutes when the cavalry arrived.

She made her way around the left side of the church where the graveyard was located. Clements had said something about a broken grave – it was probably a long shot, but worth checking out. It was not difficult to locate, and as Lavache had hoped was the case, lay directly below the window to the side chapel, where Rotunda Wells had met her fate.

Not for the first time, Lavache applauded her own fashion choice to wear steel toe-capped boots, as she kicked at the loose corner of the grave. The poor sod had been dead two hundred years; there was no likelihood his family would sue her for desecration of the family burial plot. The concrete at the edge crumbled but did not yield further. Lavache grimaced. Aware that she was being watched, she decided to wait until uniform arrived to cordon off the scene before exploring further.

She considered the area. There was clear evidence that some foliage had been dislodged around the area and the grass looked flattened around the grave. There were no fresh flowers around the headstone, therefore nothing to suggest the grave had been recently visited by family members – and it would have been a very diligent mourner, in any case, to still be bringing flowers to the grave of Ebenezer Montfichet, b. 1767, d. 1819.

Once the SOCOS plus back up had arrived from the local station and Hollingham CID, Lavache arranged for a screen to be erected around the dilapidated gravestone and surrounding foliage. Nabbing one of the more buff Scenes of Crime Officers for assistance, she succeeded in jemmying open the grave with a crowbar without his help. The heavy concrete slab now to one side, Lavache felt her heart beat faster as her suspicions were confirmed.

She shone her torchlight, picking out the top of a stepladder. Yes, there was no doubt about it. The remains of Ebenezer Montfichet had been removed. This was how the killer had escaped.

"Don't go anywhere and don't let anyone inside the tent, I'm going down," Lavache instructed the male SOCO.

Testing the ladder that was propped up against the inside of the grave, Lavache gingerly descended backwards into the abyss, torch in mouth. Her feet landed on some well-established flagstones, which appeared to have been placed on the floor at the bottom of the shaft some time ago.

She shone her torchlight. About six feet in front of her, directly below the headstone, which was almost flush against the side wall of the church, was a small wooden door. It was bolted from the outside but not locked. Lavache slid the bolt across with ease, suggesting it was in regular use. Stooping, she found herself in a small space the size of a hall cupboard. She propped the door open, to allow the light from the open grave to pour in. Above her head was a sliding hatch. It pushed open easily when she applied pressure with her hand. The drag marks on the flagstones suggested the ladder was required to enter the hatch, so Lavache fetched it and propped it up against the stone wall foundations of the church below ground level. She ascended the ladder, by now having guessed that she would emerge somewhere inside the side chapel.

On climbing a few rungs, Lavache immediately found her head surrounded by fabric. She shone the torch. They were ecclesiastical garments. Aha…. so that was how the murderer had done it!

9

"Boss, where have you been, we've been looking for you everywhere!" Sienna Jones exclaimed, as Lavache appeared in the front foyer of the church. As instructed, the graveside SOCO had kept Lavache's whereabouts to himself. It was vital the killer did not get wind of Lavache's discovery of their getaway route. One careless word from an officer, in front of the members of the public congregating outside, would be enough to give the murderer a head start.

"What's going on then?" Lavache asked, avoiding the question.

"Scenes of Crime confirm Harvey Green was most likely stabbed in the back with the same knife that was used to kill Rotunda Wells. He had his back to the killer, so death would have been instantaneous, hence the shocked expression on his face. Next of kin have been informed – he's widowed, so that's his son and daughter."

"No sign of the murder weapon?" Lavache enquired.

"Nope. And no footprints either. Nobody saw anyone leave the building, so again it's as if the killer vanished into thin air."

Or underground, Lavache thought to herself. "So, no witnesses?"

"Nope. The pathologist estimates the time of death as between nine and ten a.m."

"But what would the motive be?" Sienna wondered. "Is this a homophobia thing, boss, do you reckon? A lesbian is murdered and then the minister who agreed to marry them is stabbed, too?"

"It would look that way, I agree," Lavache nodded, keeping her cards close to her chest. There was still some information she needed before she was willing to share her thoughts with the team.

They were interrupted by Kaur.

"Boss, there's woman from the Post Office wants to speak to you. Says it's urgent."

"Well, bring her in," Lavache replied impatiently.

"She's over the road in the Post Office, boss. She says she can't leave it unattended."

"She can close the shop briefly to speak to the police; they can just wait for their sodding pensions!"

"It's not that boss, she's got a disabled son – he's actually the witness."

"For ferk sake!" Lavache scowled. "Can't you deal with it, Kaur?" What a ferkin waste of space this kid was.

"She's insisting on you, boss."

Lavache took the Lord's name in vain then steered Sienna outside with her.

"Not a word, Jones, but can you be on standby in ten minutes. I may need you with me. You're the only one of these ferkin' jokers I can rely on."

Sienna nodded, pride and excitement welling up inside. *She knows who's done it*, she clocked.

Milton Welby Post Office was around the corner, almost directly opposite the temporary tent set up around the open grave of Ebenezer Montfichet.

The postmistress was short and middle-aged with greasy highlighted hair and a careworn expression. In short, she looked like the majority of fifty something lower middle class women in the UK.

"Inspector Lavish, I'm Jennifer Bucky. My boy's upstairs."

Lavache couldn't be bothered to correct her. She followed the postmistress up the backstairs to a rather grubby living room above the shop, where a quadriplegic young man somewhere in his twenties sat in a wheelchair near the window. He had a bib on which was soggy from dribble, and what looked like porridge, Lavache noted with barely disguised disdain. Empathy was entirely absent from her scantly furnished portfolio of social skills. She wondered how he got downstairs. Perhaps there was a stairlift of some sort in the back of the house.

"This is Dale, Inspector. He can't speak, that's why I need to be here."

Great, Lavache moaned inwardly. This was going to be one great big ferkin waste of time.

"You said your son had something to tell me – so to speak," Lavache commented impatiently and tactlessly, in true style.

"Well, it's the funniest thing, Inspector, but…"

"It's Detective Chief Inspector, but carry on."

"Sorry, Inspector, I mean Detective Chief… anyway, when you were on the telly the other night, after that girl was murdered, Dale here started going nuts and asking me to put his favourite video on."

"Video?" Lavache frowned. Did anyone still use VCRs these days? Mind you, this was Milton Welby. And the Post Office did look like something straight out of Foyle's ferkin War.

"Then again, this morning, he does the same thing. About 9.30. I was just sorting the magazines when he starts yelling from upstairs. So I goes up and he's pointing out the window over to the church."

"Go on," Lavache said eagerly, listening now.

"But all I can see is that daft fella with his binbag walking out the church yard."

"The Sockman?"

"That's the one."

"What direction was he walking – away from the church?"

"That's right, down the side by the graves and out the back gate. Lost weight, mind you. Haven't seen him all this week, think maybe he's been poorly or something. Or maybe he was scared – you lot been looking for him all week, aintcha?"

"He could be a valuable witness," Lavache replied.

"But you surely don't think he did it, do you?" Jennifer frowned. "I mean he's half a sandwich short, but he's harmless enough. Lives in an old shed at Nolton allotments."

"We know," Lavache replied, not revealing that the Sockman hadn't been seen at Nolton Welby allotments all week.

"Then Dale starts pointing at his blasted video again and that's when I decided I had to speak to you, Detective Inspector."

Lavache looked confused. "What's the video got to do with it? Your son spotted the Sockman and that's good to know, as we've been looking for him, but couldn't you have just told my Constable that? I'm very busy – this is a murder enquiry, Miss Bucky."

"It's Mrs."

"Whatever…. What the ferk?"

Jennifer Bucky stood back triumphantly as she pressed play on an exceedingly blurry and wobbly copy of Michael Jackson's Thriller video. Dale started making loud groaning noises and banging his head excitedly against the headrest of his motorised wheelchair as the video got to the scene where several corpses emerged from a grave.

Now Lavache knew for sure her hunch was right. Now all she needed was the evidence.

"Thank you, Miss Bucky. Thank you, Dave. You did the right thing."

And with that, Lavache turned on her heels and ran down the stairs, summoning Jones to meet her outside.

"Shipton Welby, School Row, blue lights," Lavache barked, jumping into the passenger seat of

Jones's silver Mercedes A-Class. She barked some further instructions to Oakes and Clements on her mobile. Kaur could guard the corpse until Forensics were finished. That was about all she was good for, ferkin' useless waste of space. Who knows, Kaur might even learn something from the dead body!

10

Lavache had to wait until the next morning for her Poirot moment in the sun. It had taken several hours to round up the killer, who was eventually detained at Clapham Junction station. And then she had to wait for tests to come back from Forensics. The Sockman had been located with a bloodstained neckerchief in his pocket, the blood type a clear match for both Harvey Green and Rotunda Wells. Further investigations had uncovered the murder weapon, an expensive Japanese chef's knife, wrapped up in a mud-splattered men's shirt inside his binbag of discarded clothing.

The incident room at Hollingham CID instantly fell silent as Lavache entered the room, flanked by the Chief Constable and his deputy.

"Good morning. I'm pleased to confirm that we have secured the arrest of the killer of Rotunda Wells and Harvey Green and they are currently locked up at Clapham Town Police Station, awaiting transfer to County HQ."

"So, the Sockman did it after all?" Kaur enquired, who had been left out of the loop as Lavache wouldn't have trusted her to catch a cold, let alone a killer.

"If you're referring to the theft of three pairs of Y-fronts, a pair of blue jeans and two shirts from the pub landlord's washing line, then yes, the Sockman did it," Lavache replied, surveying the room and enjoying the rapt attention of her fellow colleagues and senior officers.

"However, if you're referring to the murder of Rotunda Wells and the Reverend Harvey Green, then no, the Sockman – or Terry O'Hague to give his real name – is not guilty. The murderer – or should I say, murderess – is the Reverend Karen Dervish. We now have concrete evidence linking her to both murders." *Quite literally*, Lavache thought to herself.

"For the benefit of Detective Constable Kaur and to fully debrief the Chief Constable, I've requested DCI Lavache presents the case," Deputy Chief Constable Michael Stewart informed those present.

Lavache cleared her throat and swigged from a large pint glass of water.

"The case began when Rotunda Wells was stabbed in the back shortly before her own wedding ceremony, in the side chapel of Milton Welby Unitarian Church. The only person who could physically have done it, according to the information we were provided with by witnesses, was her father, Nigel Wells. However, he had no motive and seemed genuinely devastated. Despite extensive searches of his house and the local area, we couldn't find a murder weapon. It looked like the most likely explanation was a homophobic crank or some jealous ex-lover had somehow snuck into the building unnoticed and taken their chances when Nigel nipped out to the loo. However, the Reverend Green insisted he would have noticed anyone enter the church from his position behind the altar. And besides, that person would have been taking a hell of a risk – how could they have known that the father of the bride would need the toilet in that short window between waiting in the chapel and walking up the side nave to the altar?"

"I toyed with the idea that somebody might have been lying in wait in the side chapel beforehand, but they would have been seen by Nigel unless they hid in the cupboard and in any case, how could they possibly have escaped, once Nigel raised the alarm? The Minister had a full view of the one and only entrance to the church and would have seen anyone else enter or exit. He didn't and according to all and sundry, he was a truthful man, an old school man of his word and I certainly had that impression, too. And though I say it myself, I'm a ferkin good judge of character."

She just can't help herself, Sienna Jones thought, winking at Gary Oakes.

"I'll be honest, I was as puzzled as the rest of you as how the murder could have been committed, if it wasn't Nigel Wells himself. It wasn't really until Clements here mentioned stubbing his toe on the corner of a broken gravestone in the churchyard that a crazy idea entered my head – but I'll return to that in a minute. I went to the church with Clements with the intention of inspecting the gravestone, when we came across Harvey Green's body in the admin office. There was a tiny piece of cream paper lodged under his forehead, that the murderer had obviously overlooked, when removing a document from under his head. What was this document, and why was it so important that we couldn't see it?"

Lavache paused to zoom in on the fragment of cream paper on the whiteboard on the wall.

"If you look closely, you'll see the word Rob just on the right-hand edge. It's the start of Robert Webb & Co's business address. They were the architects drawing up the plans for the building works at the church. That was why Harvey Green went to a buildings committee meeting instead of taking marriage classes with Rotunda Wells and Phoebe Toser."

Lavache paused to take a sip of water.

"Now, several things struck me as odd here. Firstly, as Clements here brought to my attention – " Lavache nodded in acknowledgement to the Detective Constable, "Why was the Church having renovations done, when the building looks in fairly good condition and the congregation is pretty small? And secondly, why did Karen Dervish not take the wedding service, when she had run the marriage classes and knew the couple, and was also – by all accounts – someone who liked the limelight and wanted the kudos of officiating at a lesbian wedding?"

"When I visited Harvey Green at his house, he was looking at the building plans for the church, the same ones that he was looking at when he was murdered. He also had an email up on his computer which I took the liberty of reading when he went to get us some drinks. It mentioned digging below the foundations to create some underfloor heating. So, it wasn't renovation work as such, just installing a new heating system, which affected the fabric of the building. This is complicated legally, because the building still belongs to the Church of England. So, Green had to go to these meetings, rather than the Associate Minister or a lay member of the church, because it was a sensitive issue requiring his presence, aas a figurehead, rather than because it was a huge building project. These meetings were on a Tuesday, which clashed with marriage classes, hence Karen Dervish took the class instead."

"It struck me as very odd – as it did Harvey Green – that Karen should make herself unavailable on the day of Phoebe and Rotunda's wedding, especially when she had been milking the media limelight over hosting Milton Welby's first lesbian wedding. She'd got her picture in the Herald and the Chronicle already. It was especially odd, since all she was doing was visiting her aunt in Shipton Welby, which she arguably could have done any time. I had a sense she was involved in some capacity, but couldn't see how she could be in the vicinity of the church on the day of the wedding, despite having access to the building, as she had an alibi for the time of death. Karen's aunt, Lottie Widdecombe, had confirmed to Jake that Karen had arrived at 10.30 a.m. with some shopping for her. Jake, do you want to take it from here?"

"It's Jack, boss."

11

Clements cleared his throat nervously and stood up. "When I visited the aunt's house to check up on Karen's alibi, I noticed a few things. I didn't put them in my notes, because they didn't seem relevant at the time, but afterwards I realised they might be, so I messaged the boss yesterday morning, after we'd found Harvey Green's body."

"And I'm glad you did, Jake," Lavache butted in, "Because you confirmed what I was suspecting. So next time, put every single little thing you can think of in your notes, 'cos you never know where it might lead. We've had a couple of issues of this lately, haven't we, Jake?"

"Yes, boss," Clements nodded, blushing furiously. "Erm yeah, so…" He consulted his notes nervously.

"What sort of things, *Jack*?" Sienna asked, coming to his rescue, where Lavache had knocked him off stride with her intervention. Oakes grinned at her emphasis on the young constable's correct first name, exaggerated further by her strong Welsh accent.

"So, when I went to the old girl's house, there were just a few little exchanges between Karen and her aunt. I didn't think much of them – just the typical sort of conversations between old people who are losing it a bit, and younger family members. Lottie accused Karen of having pinched some of her stuff from the kitchen and moving her stuff around. My nan got like that before she died, accusing my mum of all sorts, so as I said, I didn't think to note it down. But with hindsight, there was nothing remotely dotty about Lottie…."

Oakes and Jones laughed and Lavache glared at them.

"She had a right go at Karen about moving her mantlepiece clock. Karen told her not be so daft and changed the subject. But I looked at the clock on the way out, and there was a non-dusty rectangle on the mantlepiece, where it looked like the clock had stood previously, but it had been moved two or three inches. Stupid of me, with hindsight, not to note it down – I didn't even look at the time on it – but I just didn't clock it at the time."

Lavache directed a further glare at Oakes as he snorted into his coffee cup at Clements' unintended pun.

"I don't get it," Kaur frowned.

She would have to go, Lavache told herself.

"Karen had obviously tampered with the clock and put it back an hour, Mandeep," Lavache explained in the tone of voice one would use with a very young child. "Thereby making it look to the aunt that she had arrived at 10.30 instead of 11.30. She probably amended the clock sometime after, but unfortunately, didn't put the clock back in the exact spot she'd found it. The old lady noticed. Unfortunately, Jake didn't notice at the time, or if the clock was still an hour out." Lavache rolled her eyes.

"Sorry, boss," Clements mumbled. It felt that no matter how hard he tried, the bar was always set too high. It was a feeling shared by his numerous predecessors at Hollingham CID.

"Never mind, lad, you did well," the Deputy Chief Constable smiled at him, who was also a friend of Neville Clements. That DCI really was a frightful bully. Maybe it was her turn to go out on secondment – he'd heard Northumbria Constabulary were particularly short-staffed at present.

"So," Lavache took over again, "The clock anecdote confirmed my suspicions as to who our murderer was, alongside the accusation that items had gone missing from Lottie's kitchen. I would bet my life on it that a large chef's knife had gone missing – and when Sienna and I visited Lottie yesterday, she confirmed this."

"I get that, but I still don't get *how* the Associate Minister did it," Kaur frowned. "Did she float through the walls of the church?"

"Almost," Lavache replied. "So, going back to the graveyard, Jake here had told me about a broken gravestone. We were side-tracked by finding Harvey Green's body, but what I had actually intended doing, was examining this gravestone. Once the team arrived at the crime scene, I took the opportunity to inspect the grave. It was, as I suspected, directly outside the side chapel wall. With the help of Laurence from Scenes of Crime, I cordoned off the area. I opened up the grave and found, instead of earth and some old bones, a void about six feet deep with some ladders. I went down with a torch and discovered it had been dug out some time ago – goodness knows why, maybe something to do with those ferkin' priest holes they always bang on about in *Midsomer Murders*. I was able to proceed about six feet further before finding myself in a cupboard shaped room with a wooden hatch above. When I pushed on the hatch, it opened easily. I needed to move the ladders to climb up into the hatch. I then found myself surrounded by vicar frocks and realised I was in the cupboard in the side chapel. From there it became obvious how Karen Dervish managed to enter and escape the building without being seen. Last Saturday, she'd entered the church via the grave early in the morning then waited in the grave shaft, then later in the cupboard, waiting for her chance to stab Rotunda Wells. Karen knew, because she'd taken the marriage classes, that Nigel Wells had a weak bladder. Rotunda had made some comment to her during their conversations about her father needing to go to the loo every ten seconds when he was nervous – we got the whole story out of her last night. So, Karen could more or less bank on having two minutes alone with Rotunda. And predictably, she did. Dervish took her chance expertly then disappeared back inside the cupboard and down the grave shaft. She then returned to her car dressed as the Sockman, got changed somewhere and drove to her aunt's."

Kaur swore to a significant extent then put her hand over her mouth, realising she was in the presence of the Chief Constable and his deputy.

"Unfortunately for Karen, she *was* seen – on both occasions," Lavache added, then paused for dramatic effect.

"The Post Office is opposite the graveyard. The postmistress, Jennifer Bucky, has a paraplegic son, Dave, who spends most of his day, from dawn till dusk, looking out the upstairs window, which faces onto the graveyard. When Harvey Green was found dead yesterday, Jennifer asked to speak to me. She told me that Dave had gone mental in his wheelchair yesterday morning at about half nine. By the time Jennifer got herself upstairs and realised he had seen something, she had missed what had happened. But she did catch sight of our resident village idiot, the Sockman, leaving the back of the church. But crucially, she made a comment that the Sockman appeared to have lost weight. She also told me that Dave had insisted she put on his favourite video, Michael Jackson's *Thriller*, and in particular, the gory scene where a corpse climbs out of a grave."

Kaur clasped her hand over her mouth.

"Jennifer mentioned that he'd done exactly the same thing last Saturday – when Rotunda Wells was stabbed. And of course, the only person spotted near the church at the time of Rotunda's murder, was – "

"The Sockman!" Kaur called out, enlightenment spreading across her thin face. Then she frowned again. "But I thought you said the Associate Minister did it…"

Oakes slapped his forehead.

"She disguised herself as the Sockman, Mandeep," Jones explained. "That's why Jennifer Bucky commented that he appeared to have lost weight. It wasn't him. It was Karen Dervish. She's quite big for a woman, and certainly strong enough to lift a gravestone or stab someone with force, but not stocky like *the Sock*."

"But I don't get what her motive was – she obviously wasn't homophobic, cos she did their marriage classes," Kaur frowned.

"That was troubling me as well, Kaur," Lavache took over again. "While it made sense in some ways – Dervish was strangely unavailable for the wedding ceremony, yet in the area – I couldn't see an obvious motive. It was only yesterday, when we gained access to her house, that it became clear. Most of you haven't seen these images yet, either."

Lavache clicked on a selection of photos taken at Dervish's two-bedroom house in Nolton Welby.

"This is what we found in her spare room." Lavache used her infrared pointer to indicate a pin board with newspaper clippings attached. The clippings contained headlines of murders that had taken place in churches over the years. There was a pause as everyone screwed their eyes to read the slightly fuzzy headlines on the newspaper clips.

"Black tourism," Lavache enlightened the room. "All of these churches where murders occurred have become places of pilgrimage for so-called black tourists. Nothing to do with skin colour, before you set the Woke Brigade on me. These churches make a killing in visiting trade, pardon the pun, especially during the summer months. Some of them even stock macabre souvenirs for sale and run tours of the murder sites. It can be a real money spinner for small rural churches – which is naturally a real ego boost for the clergy employed therein, who are often under real pressure to get bums on seats and pennies in the collection box. We even found cuttings from bookstore catalogues and online stores of books that had been published on the subject."

"So Dervish was trying to raise money for the church?" Kaur looked perplexed.

"I would say Karen Dervish was trying to elevate her own profile – remember how eager she was to speak to the press about the church's first ever same-sex wedding? The articles were more about her role in Rotunda and Phoebe's nuptials than about the couple themselves. This was a distinctly unremarkable middle-aged woman who longed for recognition and took desperate measures to achieve it. She had lost all perspective and sense of reality – probably from living alone for many years. That was certainly the impression Jones and I got from interviewing her in the early hours of this morning. Sienna do you want to take over?"

"Certainly, boss," Jones replied, only too pleased to make an impression in front of the Chief Constable and Deputy Chief Constable.

"Dervish thought she was going to get away with both murders, that nobody would ever work out how she did it. This would steep the church in mystery and a degree of notoriety and thereby bring fame to the church, and by extension, herself. She intended being right in the thick of it, when the press inevitably came calling. She seemed to have a narcissistic desire to be the centre of attention. She was probably starved of it as a child, as we discovered her parents died in a car crash and Karen was passed around foster carers before being taken in by her aunt, Lottie Widdecombe, as an older teenager. We can see even in her dotage that Lottie is a forceful character and would have soon squashed any personality out of Karen. Karen was rather non-descript in manner and appearance, which some of the witnesses commented on during our initial questioning at the church, following the murder of Rotunda Wells. She was in the shadow of the incisive and well-respected Harvey Green and seemed to crave more limelight."

"Unfortunately, Karen didn't bank on Dale Bucky seeing her from the Post Office window. She also hadn't foreseen – because Harvey Green hadn't spoken to her about it in any great depth – that installing underfloor heating would require architect plans to be drawn up. Presumably Harvey had run those plans by her one day this week – remember the boss saw him looking at them in his study – and she'd realised her underground getaway would be discovered. So, Green had to go. She presumably followed him to the church yesterday morning and seized her opportunity. It was pretty early in the morning for a sleepy place like Milton Welby and she took her chances that she wouldn't be seen – or even if she was, she was disguised as the Sockman in any case. But unfortunately for her, Dale was at his usual post and saw her emerge from the grave. I suspect she pushed the gravestone across first and entered the church that way, too, in order to catch Green unawares, as he would have seen her through the office window if she'd let herself in the front."

"But wasn't she taking an almighty risk of being seen and apprehended, all the same?" Oakes commented sceptically. Though Dervish had been arrested for the murders, he still found it all incredibly far-fetched and almost beyond belief, like some traditional English television crime caper aimed at an international market.

"She made sure it was very overgrown in that area of the churchyard – she was responsible for the church exterior, after all – so that it wouldn't be obvious exactly what was going on. Plus, people are used to the Sockman ambling around the graveyard looking for old clothes. It's the top spot in Milton Welby for a drunken shag once the pubs have shut – hence plenty discarded items of clothing. We also found a spade hidden in undergrowth behind the headstone that she used to prize open the grave, containing traces of blood. While Karen was careful to wear gloves, some blood from her Sockman disguise must have rubbed off on the spade. The blood matches that of Harvey Green and Rotunda Wells."

The Deputy Chief Constable whistled. "This is really quite unbelievable."

"Tell me about it," Sienna Jones concurred.

"So, what did she do with the Sockman?" the Deputy Chief Constable enquired. "Bribed him to stay away from the area last week?"

"That would've been too risky. The Sockman isn't the full picnic, so to speak. She lured him into her car on some pretext then drugged him and tied him up in her auntie's shed at the bottom of the old lady's massive garden in Shipton, Sir," Jones replied. "We found him yesterday. She had at least left him some water and Hobnobs and enough slack on the rope for him to feed himself − so, a smattering of Christian compassion. He's now back on his feet and can be seen at a rotary airer near you."

The team chuckled.

"So, what will happen to Karen Dervish now?" Oakes wondered.

"She'll get her fifteen minutes of fame, then be locked away for a very long time, I should think," Lavache replied.

"So, about five years, then?" Oakes replied cynically. He was shot a furious glare by the Chief

Constable. It was not the best example to set in front of young, impressionable officers such as Clements and Kaur.

12

Lavache stretched out her long, lithe limbs in her king-size bed the following morning. It had been an action-packed and adrenalin-filled 48 hours and she had been granted a day off to recover from the events of the past few days. Her mobile phone pinged.

She frowned. She had turned all her work notifications off to enable her to catch up on some much-needed sleep. Who could this be? She didn't have many friends and her family all hated her.

It was from the auction site…. Shit! The rowing machine! Lavache hastily scrolled down to her messages. The good news was that the seller, HottieHels90, had not relisted the rower. The bad news was, HottieHels wanted her to pick it up by noon or she would put it up for auction again.

Lavache swore. The absolute last thing she felt like doing was driving across the border into Berkshire to manoeuvre some heavy machinery into the back of her car. But then again, where would she get that particular model at that price again?

Her stinginess, fitness obsession and innate drive won out over her desire to sleep. She could go back to bed afterwards, she reasoned, whereas the rowing machine would not wait.

"Ferkin hell!" Lavache exclaimed, pulling up outside a smart red brick detached house with fake colonnades. Normally she would have thought nothing of dumping her car on the driveway. But for some reason, she felt nervous. Work had never taken her near this swanky new estate just outside of Newbury. So Lavache left her car in the road and walked cautiously up the driveway in her usual figure-hugging black ensemble of skinny jeans, V-neck t-shirt and biker boots.

Lavache pressed the doorbell, feeling her heart beating faster as she waited for a silhouette to appear behind the opaque door. And it was worth waiting for.

"HottyHels?" Lavache enquired, her voice breaking slightly as she took in a whitewashed version of herself. HottyHels stood at around 5'10, with high cheekbones and short-cropped white blonde hair. Her lithe body was encased in a tight-fitting white t-shirt and white Levi's. Only her suntanned bare feet differentiated her from Lavache in terms of apparel.

"You must be DCI Lavache," HottyHels grinned, extending a slim, well-manicured hand. "Helen Beresford."

"You can call me Lou," Lavache said awkwardly, feeling her voice crack slightly. *What is wrong with me?*

"You might want to reverse up the driveway – Lou – the rower's pretty heavy."

"Uh, yeah, didn't think of that," Lavache mumbled. Was it her imagination, or was this blonde fitness goddess staring at her bum as she walked back to her car?

"It's in the back room," Helen indicated as Lavache returned. She followed *HottyHels* through an enormous high gloss kitchen, complete with marble topped island, to a large conservatory type edifice.

"So why are you selling it?" Lavache asked the obligatory question.

"Got a better one," Helen replied, shrugging nonchalantly, as if she were replacing a faulty kettle. Lavache would have loved to have this kind of money. What on earth did HottyHels do for a living? There was probably a rich fella in the background, Lavache thought cynically.

"Do you want to try it out?" Helen enquired.

"Uh, sure," Lavache stuttered. It was a completely reasonable suggestion, given she was about to part with the best part of two hundred pounds in cash.

Wishing she'd worn her black Nikes, Lavache sat self-consciously on the rowing machine and reached forward for the handles, her well-muscled forearms tensing as she thrust backwards and pulled the wire rope towards her flat chest.

"Seems pretty smooth," she commented, trying to sound nonchalant as she stepped off. She took her black leather wallet out of her back pocket and held out a folded wad of notes. Helen didn't even bother counting them, tossing the notes casually on the speckled marble worktop, as if it were loose change to tip the cleaner at Christmas.

"So, let's get this beast in your car. Got the seats down already?"

Helen was so damn smooth and calm, Lavache thought, while for some inexplicable reason, she felt like a quivering wreck. What the ferk was wrong with her? She had never felt cowed in another person's presence like this. She took the lighter back end of the rower and followed Helen meekly out to her own car.

Lavache slammed the boot shut, once the equipment was carefully manoeuvred into her Jeep.

"Well, thanks," she said awkwardly.

Helen held a smooth, long-fingered hand out to shake. Lavache looked away. Much to her absolute mortification, she could feel tears brimming behind her eyes. *What the hell was going on?*

"It's been a tough week, huh?" the other woman asked gently, her soothing tone at odds with her sinewy. Lavache just shook her head, turning her back to Helen, deeply embarrassed and in total confusion as to what had come over her.

Lavache covered her face with her hands as tears spilled down her high cheekbones. It was if the ice was melting, that everything she had held tightly inside for all of her life thus far had suddenly decided to spill out of the confines of her body. She felt totally and utterly out of control. And it was terrifying.

Lavache felt powerless to resist as the blonde woman wrapped her arms around her and hugged her tightly to her slim but taut frame. Lavache took her hands away from her eyes and held on for dear life, wrapping her arms around Helen's back and resting her chin on her shoulder, sobbing uncontrollably. She couldn't remember the last time she had cried like this – not since primary school, when the pretty popular girls had teased her about her boyish appearance. She had vowed then, at age seven. never again to expose her vulnerabilities.

"You better come back in," Helen murmured after a few moments had elapsed. She steered Lavache back indoors.

But this time, she took her upstairs.

About the author

Carol A Shepherd is an author, college lecturer and LGBT faith activist from Eastleigh, near Southampton, UK. You can find her books at www.carolshepherdbooks.info

If you valued this book, the author would greatly appreciate a review to spread the word and support independent publishers.

You can also subscribe to Carol's newsletter, The Bi Christian Writer

https://www.subscribepage.com/bichristianwriter

More titles from Easy Yoke Publishing can be found at www.easyyoke.org

By the same author

From Easy Yoke Publishing

Death by Peanuts
The Allotment Affair
You Shop You Drop

Hunt 6

Death by Peanuts

Acne-ridden Christian detective, Mark 'Pizza' Parlour, must find the killer among his own congregation when an ex-serviceman slumps head-first into a plate of chocolate éclairs at the Church Council meeting. But the murderer appears to have ascended into thin air. This is the first in the DI 'Pizza' Parlour series.

303 pages, ISBN 9781838162047

Easy Yoke Publishing, UK

The Allotment Affair

Acne-ridden Christian detective, Mark 'Pizza' Parlour, must dig deep to weed out the allotment killer. Salik Gani is suspected of murder, when Davidson Munroe, a prominent member of the BASC (British Alliance of Senior Citizens) is poisoned with a lethal dose of paraquat! This is the second in the DI 'Pizza' Parlour series.

284 pages, ISBN 9781838162054

Easy Yoke Publishing, UK

You Shop You Drop

Acne-ridden Christian detective, Mark 'Pizza' Parlour, must investigate the kidnapping of three Yummy Mummies in South Hampshire. A quirky ransom note requests that 50k is left in a Cornflakes box near a local high-rise. Will Parlour unmask the potential Cereal killer before the women meet their grisly fate? This is the third in the DI 'Pizza' Parlour series.

230 pages, ISBN 9781838162061

Easy Yoke Publishing, UK

Hunt 6

Gay physio Broosky hopes to entice club captain Nathan out of the closet and onto his massage table. But when a sex abuse scandal hits the football club and a youth player is found dead in the club showers, Brooksy fears the chances of Nathan coming out are zero.

160 pages, ISBN 9781838162030

Easy Yoke Publishing, UK